The Ghost

Of

Henry Sch

An intriguing tale of greed, love, … geance and the paranormal.

By

Angela L Garratt

To Andy

Never give up
on your dreams

Love

Angela Garratt.

To my partner, Niven, who has perpetually put up with the constant tapping of keys, even when he is trying to sleep.

Table of Contents

Part One

Unity

Jecepi picked up the morning newspaper and put it on the table in his modest little book shop, which was situated on the corner of Greeley town centre opposite the newly opened clock tower. Marketers' every morning would pop their head around the door or tilt their hats to say hello to Jecepi. He was a well loved and respected man, a God fearing man, and his two loves in his life was his shop and his cat, Benny. Horse and carts would almost fly past the windows of the local shops and on those cobbled streets anything could happen. People had been killed before now and as it happens that is exactly what the headline of the news paper stated.

25th November 1856

Greeley News

Accident on Lower High Street

The body of a young man aged 17 years old was found dead yesterday near the entrance of Lower High Street, Greeley. The boy, who we can not name for legal reasons, had died with severe head injuries. It is believed by police that this death is the result of a horse and cart accident, no further inquiries are being made by the police…

Jecepi could not bring himself to read anymore, he knew full well that young boy didn't die by any coach accident. He and the rest of Greeley knew it was the work of Henry Schnieber. That poor boy, Jecepi knew his name was John Tullin and was defending his mother when Henry came sniffing round for money. Protection money he called it. Said, 'no 'arm would come to us as long as we shop keepers' kept paying up.'

Mr and Mrs Tullin ran the local cobblers down there on Lower high street. Business was slow for them these days; no one could afford to be able to get their shoes done once Henry Schnieber got his claws into them. In fact, it was that same reason that Jecepi himself was finding it hard too. Who can afford to buy a book when all their money is taken away from them? Most people around here can hardly afford to breathe let alone read.

The day went by quickly, his accounting had been done and so had his stock taking. There wasn't much difference from the weeks previous, like I said, not too many books were bought by people these days.

"You hungry Benny? c'mon, let's get home then." Jecepi muttered to his tabby cat. He felt his shoulders relax with a little sigh; he knew that talking to a cat was not the sanest thing in the world to do. But Benny was the only being in the whole of Jecepi's world that would listen intently to him, when he needed some one to talk to.

The clouds were dark and the nights were drawing in. The sun had set by 5pm and tonight it was raining. Jecepi winced at the weather; he didn't want to catch a chill; he would still have to work ill or not, his old bones were already grinding him down and he did not want to add to his pain. Henry Schnienber would not wait for his 'protection money.' Before leaving the warm and dry safety of his little book shop, he took a deep breath and wondered how the world had become such a cruel place. So, after snuffing out the gas lamp and locking up, Benny followed Jecepi all the way home.

Thankfully though, home was not too far away. Kings Hill, about a twenty minute walk away from the shop. A beautiful, old church stood on the very top of the hill. The Black Church, locals called it. Not because it is evil or sinister, but because it has been standing there on that hill for that long the brick work has actually turned black. There are graves on that church yard from the sixteenth century. Jecepi loved it, loved the grounds, the view from the hill top and everything that the church stood for. It was the church and his faith in God that made him feel safe in this terrible and scary world.

Benny was still by Jecepi's side when he came to his own front door, encircling his ankles and almost tripping him up as he entered his cold, yet soon be warm home. Benny ran straight for his bed which was situated right next to the burned out but still warm embers of last nights fire. Once he was settled, he started to wash himself with his rough, sandpaper tongue that acted as a brush on his relatively long and seemingly delicate fur.

Jecepi lit the candle's in his house; the flames flickered with the drafts that came from the edges of the door frame and the old sash windows. He then screwed up the pages of yesterday's newspaper and he lit the fire. He watched the flames dance a little bit while they caught the edges of the paper. Jecepi thought of his mother and the amount of times he had watched her do this same thing as a child; of course with Jecepi being in his 60's, 65 to be exact, his mother had died a long time ago of Influenza. His father died two years later of what everyone said was a broken heart. 'Marcus Lefetelli died because he loved his bride too much', that's what everyone said. The book shop and the family home were left to Jecepi and his cat, Benny.

Even though Jecepi was born and bred in England, his parents and their descendants were born in Naples, Italy. There was an earthquake near Mount Vesuvius and the Lefetelli family fled to England, where they thought they would be safe. Nothing ever came of that earthquake, no one died and the volcano didn't erupt, so all the panic really was over nothing.

Once the paper was alight, Jecepi lightly added the wood; the wood soon caught fire and crackled, sending sparks of lit wood up the chimney. The heat started to noticeably circulate the room. Jecepi picked up the old saucepan from the hearth, there was still some broth left from the night before and he was just about to warm it up when he heard that most dreaded sound.
A horse and cart stopped outside his house; in fact it wasn't just one horse that was attached to this cart, or in this case, coach. Only wealthy

men could afford what pulled up outside his house and there was only ever one wealthy man that ever did.
"Henry Schnieber." Jecepi muttered to himself, dreading the thought of opening the door.
Benny looked up from washing himself. The cat seemed to know that there was something wrong instantly and meowed loudly, several times. Jecepi stroked his cat, desperately trying to calm him down. He hated to see the cat in distress.
BANG! BANG! BANG! The door banged so hard, Jecepi thought it would come off its hinges.
"JECEPI, I KNOW YOU'RE IN THERE, OPEN UP OR THE NEXT PLACE I GO TO VISIT WILL BE YOUR SPLENDID LITTLE BOOK SHOP…IF YOU GET MY DRIFT."

Jecepi knew exactly what he meant. But that put him in a terrible situation. He knew he didn't have the money to pay Henry, but he also knew that if he didn't open the door he would be going back to a completely destroyed book shop tomorrow and the thought of all of those books being destroyed, all of those stories, different worlds created by different people. He couldn't say goodbye to them, it would be like saying goodbye to his family all over again. He couldn't even think about it, he knew what he had to do. He had no choice. Reluctantly, with a deep sigh, he turned the key and opened the door.

Henry Schnieber, 42 years old, heavily built with short, dark hair that suited his dark, hollow soul. He was just about to bang on the door again when the door opened. Jecepi looked up at him with fear in his eyes.

Henry had no sympathy; he didn't care if he had no money. No money, no protection. Trouble was Henry also knew that the only person Jecepi needed protecting from was Henry himself.

Benny ran out of the house, his fur just lightly skimming Jecepi's leg. The rain was coming down harder and the bitterly cold wind was howling around the houses like a small tornado.

Jecepi went to open his mouth to say something but before he could a giant fist hit him right between the eyes. His head was knocked back and though he didn't fall to the ground, his dazed expression told Henry everything he needed to know. Another second came and went and another fist hit him right under the jaw. Jecepi felt his jaw bone crack and within seconds he fell to the floor with a thump. A kick to the stomach and one last swift kick to the head, Henry Schnieber finally realised that Jecepi had had enough. He didn't want him dead; the book shop still needed to pay up and without Jecepi, the book shop would be as good as gone.

Henry walked away from the door with Jecepi bleeding from the back of his head; his weak and old stomach had caved in, causing fatal internal bleeding. He was lying on the ground, his head resting on the second step down, a drop of blood seeped though the corner of his mouth as he looked at the big old bright moon, and finally, Jecepi's eyes closed for the final time.

Benny was often fed by the neighbour's; little scrap bits of chicken and fish. His meow was well known by the people who lived in the street; after all it was loud enough. That is why Mrs Warner opened the door immediately when she heard the horse and coach leave the street and when Benny meowed at her door she knew something was wrong.

For Mrs Warner, time seemed to slow down as she called for her husband to send for Dr. Williams. She ran straight over to Jecepi and quickly assessed the situation; she took off her shawl and put it under his head. She then ran into the house and found a blanket to cover him with. She didn't know what else to do, so she just stayed with him till the doctor turned up.

~#~

It didn't take long before the neighbour's and marketer's heard about what had happened to Jecepi. He had slipped into a coma and died in hospital a few days after Mrs Warner had found him. Henry Schnieber had been terrorising people and he had used Jecepi as an example. Though the entire town was scared, they had also come to their wits end. They could not and would not put up with Henry Schnieber for much longer. They knew the only way to get rid of a bully was to stand up to him. So, Mr Warner and Dr. Williams put the word about that there was a neighbourhood meeting in the St Bartholomew's town hall this evening. They had an idea, but it was something that was not for the faint hearted. Husbands were advised to ask their wives to stay at home with their children.

They had to find a way to stop Henry, and the only way they knew how, was to kill him. But first they had to catch him and Mr Warner thought he knew how to do just that.

Seven PM on the evening of the 3rd of December, the entire male population of the town's people and some of the women too were ushered into Greeley's town hall. They knew that the best way to keep their businesses safe was to barricade the doors' but then they would have put themselves in harms way to Henry and his two henchmen. So, this was the result of the meeting.

With Dr. Williams and Mr Warner taking the roll of head chairman, they put up a vote, people who wanted to confront him, or people who want to hide and ambush him. The vote ended with 35-21 in favour of ambush.

Mr and Mrs Warner went to bed that night with a terrible feeling of anxiety for the next day, for it was planned that all shop owners and marketers would be in their shops or on their market stores as normal. However, when Henry and his boys came looking for trouble, trouble was exactly what they found. Even so, no one was expecting the terrible fate that befell Mr Schnieber, no one at all.

Part Two

War Crimes

Annie Tomkins

Annie Tomkins stood near the entrance of the underpass. The roads were rather busy for this time of the day and the sun was going down in the twilight and smog filled air. The moon was barely visible but she could see that it was full and that always made Annie nervous, for the same reason as she never did much like places such as underpasses. Her imagination was far too vivid to feel even remotely comfortable in such places. She had read too many horror novels and the full moon gave her the 'heebie jeebies' and quite rightly too, after all these are times of war, 1944 to be exact.

Annie wore quite fashionable clothes for the time. A khaki colour skirt and jacket, black shoes and stockings. She was rather proud of her stockings, they were getting harder and harder to find in this day and age. Her husband was out at war, a pilot; it scared her to death that she would one day get a telegram telling of his unfortunate but heroic death. She didn't want him to have a heroic death; she didn't want him to die at all.

Annie hung on nervously to the banister as she descended the steps. Her handbag loosely hung over her arm and her hair was up in a tight clip, though her hat covered most of it. Her breath was heavy as she took one step after the other. Her shoes quietly clicked as her low heal hit the concrete ground.

'I must be mad,' she thought out loud. She knew that this land had not always been an underpass; this one in particular was relatively new as was the busy road above it.

The underpass was warm, which was quite odd, it was freezing outside and Annie could not wait to get home to put the kettle on and finally, if her two children would let her, put her feet up. Her shoes were crippling her, rubbing away the first layer of skin on her heels. But then, something happened, she saw a light. The light was blinding and hot, oh too hot, way too hot. She knew she shouldn't have come down and my goodness me, she regretted it. But then, the light went away and there was nothing else for her to regret. Her life had been taken away from her, and she had no idea why, or who took it, everything had happened so quickly.

Annie's life had been taken from her, but her spirit remained. She looked down and saw nothing but ashes; ashes and what was left of her left hand, the hand that still wore the precious wedding ring that meant more to her than her own life. She looked to see what had happened and though she could not see anyone in particular, she saw a carriage with four horses wondering off away from her. Her spirit stood there, confused about what had just happened and why. She thought about her husband and her children; she couldn't die now; she was needed. What will become of her children? Will her husband be called out of the war? Her head was full of questions and 'what ifs'. She wanted to cry but with no body, she had no tear ducts, so she couldn't even do that. What she did want though and for some reason she knew she could, she wanted to see her children, she wanted to comfort them and hold them and tell them that everything was going to be okay, even if she didn't believe it herself. She couldn't do that latter, however, no sooner she thought of her children, she was there with them. Both of them were fast asleep. Mrs Paul was nodding off on the sofa. Mrs Paul, the next door neighbour and a very charitable lady; she didn't have a lot so she was always eager to give away her spare time to those who needed her help.

Annie's sorrow was so great; there were no words to describe just how bad she felt. She wanted so badly to hold her children, thank her neighbour and just to have her life back. But she knew that was not going to happen, not any time soon; she knew that she would be watching over them, their personal guardian angel. Annie heard a call from above, an angelic call. She knew that it was her time to go, but she would not really be gone, she would be there for them, watching, waiting and looking after them from heaven.

Maxwell Hope

Maxwell Hope came back from the front line after being wounded in action. He took a shower of bullets to his legs and spine; he almost died, but miraculously, he survived. The doctors said he would never walk again and they were right. He was stuck in that wheelchair, a chair that he hated so much, his attitude was, 'why do you need your legs to shoot a gun?' But the British Army would not let him back in. It gutted him, he was a true patriot and all he wanted to do was fight for his king and country, to follow in his fathers and his grandfather's footsteps, which had fought from the Boer War to the Great War.

Maxwell was depressed most of the time and spent a lot of time at the bar; at least he got the attention off the ladies there. He got a lot of attention of the men too, but that was more of a mutual respect, though some hated him; especially those men that were not called up in the first place, because of a medical condition of some sort or simply because of their age.

Maxwell's local was the Golden Cross and it was rather dull inside, the walls were painted brown, and the floor had floor boards covered in saw dust. The windows were blacked out and the air was full of cigarette and cigar smoke. It stunk of booze and smoke and sweat, but he sat there at a table near the bar drinking whisky. His blue eyes scanned the room and caught the eye of a pretty lady, who just happened to be the bar maid. She knew him, she had spoken to him in the past and he had asked her out for dinner before now too, but she had got a child waiting at home for her and life was difficult enough without trying to find time for herself. It's not that she didn't like him, she did and she was not so shallow to see the wheel chair as a problem like some girls did. But that made Maxwell all the more depressed, 'charming!' he thought. 'The only woman in here that really likes me and she can't find time for me.'

Maxwell hadn't got any family, he did have, but the war killed them. His mother died in a bomb explosion and his brother and best friend was killed in action; at least that is the story he was told. For all he knew he could be missing or stuck in one of those concentration camps, truth be told, he would rather him be dead than stuck in one of those places, he couldn't think of his brother in a place like that. He had heard the stories and honestly they scared him to death. His dark hair was cut into short back and sides, and was perfectly combed, he wore a suit and always took care of his appearance; he might be depressed but there was no way he was going let others know that, Maxwell was a proud man. He lit his last cigarette of the night and asked the bar maid for another whisky. He downed it in one, said his good nights and put his half smoked cigarette out in the already filled ashtray.

The night was smoggy and dank. The cobbled streets were wet and visibility was low. Maxwell found it hard to push himself along in his wheelchair, but he was determined he was not going to let it beat him, he was tired and he wanted his bed, he imagined he could hear it calling him. He crossed the road and headed towards the Greeley aqueduct. Then something caught his eye, he turned to see what it was and the street lights were one by one being extinguished; it worried him and quite rightly too. A carriage with four horses stopped next to him and with Maxwell being the curious type he stopped too, though this was to his detriment. Not even a second had passed and Maxwell, along with his wheelchair had turned to ash. All that was left was the metal frame of the chair and wheels.

Unlike Annie, Maxwell wasn't shocked or too disturbed by his death, well, not at first. After all he had regained the use of his legs. He was once again standing and then walking and jumping for joy. He had got his legs back, then he realised that the moment he finds his new love for life, his life has been taken away. He looks up to the heavens, weeps and asks, why? Why now? Then suddenly, but at the same time rather slowly, he disappears into the hands of God.

Josephine Hadley

Josephine lived on the other side of town to Annie and Maxwell. Some people referred to it as the posh part of Greeley. It was the side of town where the classes were different, not so much working class and not even upper class; she lived comfortable enough and that made her family rather snobbish. However, Josephine, only being nineteen, didn't care for snobbery. She had seen what the war had done to the town and the only thing she wanted to do was help, either that or spend most of her time walking her little dog through the neighbouring nature reserve.

Spring was definitely showing, the daffodils were up and the buds on the trees were starting to bloom. The Daisies, Buttercups and Dandelions were popping up and she loved it, everything about nature, everything comes back to life this time of year and that made her happy.

Josephine's mother was a snob, or at least that is what Josie thought of her, even calling herself Josie was unacceptable to her parents, 'you were christened Josephine, so Josephine is what you will be called!' she was continually told. She hated it.

What her mother didn't know and she felt she couldn't tell her, is that for three hours a day she volunteered at the local Hospital. Many war victims were taken there and they needed all the help they could get. Josie knew that being charitable wasn't necessarily all to do with giving money away, like her parents were constantly telling her it was. To quote her father, 'you want to help them? Give them money and let them do it all themselves.' Josie could not help but think that was a mean attitude to have, she knew that it was not money they needed to most, it was physical help. 'Charity begins at home!' they would continue to say. . .and granted, that is true, as that is written in the bible, but charity is also about helping others, regardless to whether money is involved or not. As far as Josie was concerned she kept her mind and heart open, she wanted to help in this mad world, she wanted to know that when she left it, she had contributed to it, or at least tried to and to Josie, nothing else mattered.

"Jack! Jack c'mon boy, out the way." Jack being the little wired haired terrier that she loved so dearly. Josie could hear the gallop of horses and the wheels of a cart; at first she thought that it was a bit strange, people in these parts normally have motorcars, they don't bother with the upkeep of horses, but Josie loved them, of course she did, they are beautiful and majestic animals, she owned a couple herself.

Jack complied with his orders and moved to her side. Josie then heard the gallops come to a slow and as the horse and coach stopped near her, she expected to see someone peer out and ask her a question or at least wish her a 'good day', but there was nothing of the sort. The coach didn't start again, it just stopped and the funny thing was there was no one driving it. That kind of scared her a little bit, but curiosity got the better of her; she couldn't leave without at least checking everything was okay. The whole thing just seemed odd to her. She patted the horses and they didn't seem to react, nod, or nothing, it was almost like her presence was non-existent.

Reluctantly, Josie tapped on the door of the coach and slowly it opened. Jack cowered and ran off into the bushes, poor thing was dithering with fear; he knew something wasn't right. He yapped a bark of warning. But it was too late, Josie was on the floor, her hair had suddenly turned from beautiful blonde to silver, her eyes looked shocked and wouldn't or couldn't move. What Josie saw was not the kind of thing that she could explain, not without being classed as insane.

The coach started on its way again. It disappeared into nowhere. Jack came back to Josie; he licked her stunned face, but there was no movement. Jack knew she was still alive, and until help came there was no way that Jack was going to leave her side; he lay with his head on her arm, whimpering for her to wake up again.

Eventually, help did come.

Part Three

Findings

3rd December 2006

The Greeley News

Spontaneous Human Combustion (SHC)

This is the second case in a week that two human bodies have been found, burned beyond recognition, there were no logical explanation of how the fires started. Fire crews examining the scenes are said to be baffled. Fire chief, Mr Williams said, "In Greeley's history there has never been this many cases of the unexplained phenomenon. However, Spontaneous Human Combustion was and remains to this day a matter of Myth and folklore, there has not been any actually reason to suspect that the deaths of these two people are anything other than suspicious." Detective Inspector, Jackson of Greeley Police Department said, "There are no leads at the moment, and though forensics has not found anything yet in ways of evidence, it does not mean there is nothing to find. We have got people working on this horrific scene around the clock and the two victims' have been taken to the city morgue for further examination."

George Scott Williams (22) and Louise Cartman (19), was found dead, apparently burned to death, approx. 10:15 pm last night in Dorchester Park. They were discovered by Frank Larks (43), a dog walker from a nearby street who immediately called the Police...

“Spontaneous Human Combustion, huh?” DCI Mason said as he threw the newspaper on his desk. “There are plenty of people questioning it.”

The vertical blinds moved slightly as the wind gently blew through the open window.

“I know, all those paranormal freaks scouting the place, I’ll be surprised if forensics find anything once they’ve finished poking their nose in. DI Jackson said, annoyed with the situation.

“I want you to check it out,” DCI Mason said, without a flicker in his eyes.

“What! You’re not taking this seriously, surely?” Simon asked, frustrated; he knew there was no point in arguing with the DCI, his mind had been made up, but Simon knew he was being sent on a wild goose chase.

Simon turned to leave the office, muttering to himself, “Bloody SHC, next he’ll be having me chase UFO’s, always liked the thought of tracking Bigfoot.”

DCI Mason heard him and was not impressed with his sarcasm.

“Don’t you answer me back; I have given you a job to do, now go and do it. I’ll expect the report on my desk by Monday, you hear?”

Simon sighed. He knew there was no getting out of this. He may as well just do it and get it over with. Simon smiled to himself; he wouldn’t need until Monday to get the report done; he’d probably get it all done in one night.

After leaving the office DI Simon Jackson thought that it would be a very good idea to start with searching the other cases like these that happened 25 years ago. He didn’t see the point because his heart was just not in this case. He checked them anyway, and the pictures he came across shocked the life out of him. People burned to death in parks or on the footpath near their homes. None of these cases were dissimilar from the bodies found recently. These were normal everyday places that people walked. There was no evidence to suggest that they had been moved or hidden in any way at all, though, judging by the looks of these photos, they would've be impossible to move. All they found of these bodies were ash and the charred remains of a leg, or a hand. In one case, all that was left was the right foot.

These pictures sickened Simon to the point that he was retching. He couldn't help himself, he found the wastepaper bin that was situated next to the over crowded desk, just in case he was actually sick.

The DI was concentrating so hard that he didn't hear Collette Taylor walk in; she startled him when she spoke.

"Found anything?" She asked in her soft, feminine voice. To look at her you wouldn't think that she is one of the best that CID has to offer; she doesn't even look like a police officer and that is the reason why she was considered the best. Victims and cons seem to be able to confide in her because of her gentle nature, with those blue eyes and that shoulder length blonde hair she could even fool DI Jackson, or at least she liked to think she could.

"Have you seen these photos?" He asked while half-heartedly offering her one.

"Yes, I was put on the original case back in 1986 that is why DCI Mason has assigned me to work with you on this. How could I resist?" She answered sarcastically.

DI Jackson let out a sharp breath, "ouch." He muttered.

They both smiled and carried on, examining the photos.

After about two hours of finely going through the old case files, both DI Jackson and Collette went to the local morgue. They knew they had to examine the bodies, at least what was left of them.

The drive there wasn't so bad, the traffic as per usual was enough to drive a saint to swear but, at least there was enough common sense on the roads today to ensure that most drivers' used their indicators. That was DI Simon Jackson's pet hate, the fact that many drivers these days buy cars and don't realise that indicators are built in, it annoys him so much.

"DI Jackson and this is DI Taylor, we need to see the bodies of the burn victims," DI Jackson said to the receptionist, as they pulled out their badges and pressed them to the glass that partitioned the receptionist to the DI's. The young woman that worked on the desk made an inside call to the mortician. Two minutes later the mortician met them in the waiting room and ushered the two police officers to the bodies that they had come to see.

"Well, there isn't much for you two to see, a couple of teeth and…" at this point he had pulled out the drawers, exposing the bodies to the two officers.

DI Jackson reached into the inside pocket of his suit jacket and pulled out a white handkerchief, he put it to his mouth and nose to stop himself from retching further at the sight of what was left of these charred remains.

Collette, however, walked over the foot and examined the charred ankle. The edges had been cauterized like it had been picked up and seared on a hot stove.

"Have you been able to determine the cause of the fire that killed them?"

The Mortician gave a sarcastic smile, "that's the job for the fire brigade, not us."

"C'mon, you've been doing this job for years, what d'you think what happened?" Collette asked; she looked at the Mortician with a questioning look.

"On or off the record?" He asked.

"Off!" Both Collette and Simon said simultaneously.

The Mortician raised his eyes brows and took in a deep breath. He knew that if this got out, it could be his professional reputation at stake. "As far as I can see, these people just burned up with no solid explanation. Honestly, your best bet is to try and find the witness."

"There was a witness?"

"According to your DCI there is; better still, you might want to go and talk to him, doesn't seem like he is giving you all the facts."

By this time, Collette and Simon had come to the end of referring to each other by their surnames, apart from when there was cause for it.

~#~

Simon

Simon held the door open for Collette as they walked back into the police station. She thanked him and walked through first. The station was quite bright with artificial lights, but the mosaic on the floor that showed the coat of arms for the Greeley police station was rather dull, it had been there since the opening of the police station about seventy-five years ago and needed some serious updating. To the left was the door that led to the offices, and that is where the two of them headed, this time it was Collette who opened the door for Simon and it was his turn to say 'thank you.' They smiled at one another and headed straight down the hall towards the DCI's office.

"Come in!" DCI Mason shouted as Simon knocked on the door.

"Aaarh, DI Jackson, solved the case, have you?" The DCI looked back down to finish what he was writing, and continued to utter, "That was quick!"

"NO, but it would have helped if you had of told us about the witness, who and where is it?" DI Taylor answered.

DCI Mason raised an eyebrow and looked up from his work. "You didn't ask. "She…is an homeless woman, she normally hangs out at the park, I've already spoke to her and couldn't make head nor tail about what she was saying, you want her, fine, go and get her, but don't say I didn't warn you, she'll only waste your time too."

"I think we'll be the judge of that, thank you!" Collette answered.

DCI Mason gave her a look of discontent.

“What’s her name?” Simon asked.

“June Smith. She usually pushes around a trolley full of cans, now get out my office, I’ve got useful work to do!”

~#~

Two hours and fifteen minutes later, June was found, her cans were scattered on the ground and so was her torso, neck and head up to her jaw line. Only her bottom jaw was visible, the rest of her body, legs, arms, head, they had all been burnt to ashes.

“Oh no,” Simon muttered. While putting a white cotton handkerchief to his mouth, hoping that the smell wasn’t going to make him throw up. For a DI he didn’t have much of a stomach for the dead, but then, he didn’t think that too many people did, regardless to their job.

Collette got on the radio to the police switchboard, “this is DI Taylor, 51432. Send a team of forensics to Dorchester Park; there has been another burning!” It was custom in the Greeley police department that when a crime was called in by an officer, the name and badge number had to be given first.

“On the way!” A voice muttered through the radio.

“Our only lead, what are we going to do now?”

“We can find the person who did this, we’re not gonna give up just because she’s dead!”

Just then, in the corner of Simon’s eye, he caught a glimpse of a boy. His dark skin showing in between his dark, tight braids.

As soon as Simon saw the boy he headed towards him, but the boy ran and so Simon ran after him. It didn’t take long before Simon had caught up with him and Collette had caught up with Simon.

“So what d’ya run for?”

The boy shrugged, fear ran through his eyes, he saw everything that happened, and he couldn't explain a damn thing, not without been called a liar or worse, a lunatic.

"I. . .I. . .eer, I don't know, you started chasing me, what was I supposed to do? You're not exactly dressed like a police man, how do I know who you are?" The small black boy mumbled with a shaky voice.

Simon narrowed his eyes, he wasn't buying it, he knew this boy was hiding something, Collette could feel it too.

"C'mon, we know you saw something, what d'you see?" Collette gestured to Simon to let go of him. He did, and the boy shook himself straight.

The boy sighed and rolled his eyes, shaking his head; in truth he was more scared of his mother than these police officers, he knew that if his mother had to pick him up from the police station, he would be in serious trouble. His mother was the kind to scold first and ask questions later and she scared the hell out of him. She was the reason why he never fitted in with the 'in' crowd. Just as well really, most of the kids in the area were usually looking for trouble. Plus, it wasn't just what he'd seen that bothered him, it was also what he'd found. Maybe, showing the police officers what he'd found might make it easier to explain what he'd seen; he knew what he had to do, his heart beat nineteen to the dozen and he felt sick with anxiety.

"What's ya name, boy?" Simon almost growled as he was waiting for an answer, patience wasn't one of his virtues.

"Carson Jones." Carson didn't mean to be vague, but he was truly scared, he's seen at the movies how the police try and pin murders on the people that find the body just to get a quick answer to the killings and he could see in Simon's eyes that was exactly what was running through his mind. What he didn't know is that he couldn't have been more wrong.

"I think I had better show you something before I tell you." Carson said in a shaky voice.

Suspicions intensified in Simons mind but Collette seems more intrigued than anything else.

"What have you found?" Collette asked with questioning eyes.

"Me and my brother were digging a hole in the side of the canal yesterday and we found something that looked like really old bones, we were going to go to the police and tell them but then we both thought it was best not to because we didn't want to get into any trouble." Almost like a kid with asthma, Carson took a deep breath at the end of the sentence.

Simon took in a deep breath too at the news and concern was etched all over Collette's face. For a split second, it was almost as if the sky had gone black. The last thing they wanted was another body, they just both hoped and prayed that Carson was wrong, they hoped that it was nothing more that old animal bones, but no stone could be left unturned in a murder case, they needed to see for themselves.

They could not go anywhere for the time being, they had to wait for forensics to get to the body of June Smith. It didn't take long, ten minutes and the team had started to arrive.

"Clear the area and take as many photos and samples as you can, they aint gonna get away with this!" said a very annoyed Dr Milford.

~#~

Jake

Dr Milford loved his job, he loved to see killers put away, but he hated seeing dead bodies like this, there was nothing that disturbed him more. It was almost like every murder was a personal loss to him and that is what gave him the drive to catch the killers. It was this attitude that made him the best in his field of work, a forensic scientist/artist. Jake was looked upon as a very talented man.

"Jake, we gotta go, there may be another body, were gonna go and check it out, keep us informed with what you find, we'll let you know if we need you at the other location." Simon said as Collette guided Carson to the police car.

~#~
Carson

"You'd better not be lying about this." Collette accused as she shut the back door and made her way to the passenger seat. Seconds later, Simon got in the driver's seat and started the engine, it started with a purr and Carson loved it, at fourteen years old he had a fascination with cars that would build into a future career.

Sure enough when they got to the canal side, it was discovered that Carson's claim of finding old bones was true. The bones did appear to be human, but if course this had to be confirmed. The bones didn't only look old, but they were also charred. The only way they would be able to determine how old these bones were, would be by carbon dating. Then they would have to get a forensics artist, possibly Jake, to re-invent his or hers features. Right now, there was no way of knowing either way of whom or when this person, if indeed it was a person, died.

"What on earth were you and your brother doing here in the first place, why were you digging?"

Carson gave a look of uncertainty, he wanted to tell the truth, because it was simple, but everything he had said so far, even though it was proved right, was not believed at first.

"We live in a block of flats. At first this is all he could muster. Simon looked at him as if to say, 'and?'

"We had a rabbit, it died, we needed to bury it, and we don't have a back garden."

"So when you found the bones, where did you bury it?" Colette asked, hoping to God that they didn't bury it by the remains.

"Over there," Carson pointed to a small mound that was situated right next to an old metal fence with gruesome looking spikes on top.

Both Simon and Colette gave an accepting nod to the boys answer.

"Why were you in the park today?"

Carson gave Simon a funny look, he could hear a sarcastic answer forming in his head, but under the circumstances, he decided the right answer was probably the best one.

"I was waiting for my girlfriend, Naomi." Then the sudden realisation hit him, 'I bet she is waiting there for me now,' he thought as his heart started to beat twice as fast. He really didn't want to stand her up; she wouldn't know that he was with the police. Aaarh, but what a great story to tell her when he does see her again; I mean, how often does one find a body in the middle of the park, or the canal for that matter? He can tell her that he was helping the police with their enquiries, how cool would that be? She'd be really impressed and might even like him more for it. Wow, can you imagine what they'll say in school. He'd be the talk of the town for ages, and Carson loved to be the centre of attention, providing those attentions didn't get him into trouble with his mother.

The huge smile that had just appeared on his face at the thought of telling Naomi what had happened soon disappeared at thought of telling his mother.

"Can you take me back to the park after this please?" Simon could understand the eagerness in the boy's eyes, but Carson's work wasn't over yet.

"No, you're coming to the police station; your mother'll be informed, she'll be waiting there for you. You'll need to make a formal statement; after all you're our primary witness."

Carson knew exactly what 'primary witness' and 'formal statement' meant; he had watched enough of his mom's murder mysteries.

Shortly after the forensics arrived, all three, Carson and the two police officer's made their way back to the car that was still parked nearby. Carson laughed; a bird had messed all over the windscreen. Simon didn't find it so funny, in fact, Simon was all the more annoyed by Carson's laughter. "Damn birds, need bloody shooting the bloody lot o' them." He sat there on the driver's seat trying to clean it off with sprays of water and the windscreen wipers, but the more he did it, the more it smeared and the worse it got. Carson couldn't help but laugh; he found it so funny that the more Simon was cursing at those 'damn birds' the worse it was getting. Colette had to see the funny side of it too. In the end even Simon started to laugh, but the situation wasn't getting any better. Simon got out the car, made his way over to the boot and brought out a cloth and some kind of cleaning liquid. He sprayed the windscreen and before he knew it, just as he started cleaning the glass, the rain poured down, hammering onto the car like little bullets of water. Simon looked defeated and got back in the car looking like a drowned rat and he'd only been out a matter of minutes. Carson started laughing again but the look Simon shot him was enough to shut anyone up, even Colette's smile had faded.

Simon started the car and headed off towards the police station. Carson suddenly realised that his mother was going to be there waiting for him; 'Oh good lord, no', he thought, 'I'll be grounded for a month.'

"Does my mother really have to be there?" Carson asked with trepidation.

"It's the law, your mother has to be present in order for us to be able to take your statement, besides, what you got to worry about; you're not in trouble with us, not unless there is something that you're not telling us." Simon said with quizzing eyes.

Carson frowned, "no course not, but Mom's gonna go mad, she's gonna ground me for this, I know she is." Carson pouted and sighed heavily.

Collette and Simon looked at each other with raised eyebrows. They both felt sorry for him, but there was no room for sentiment in this game, Carson being grounded really wasn't their problem.

~#~

Jake

Jakes reaction to seeing the charred bones was one of practical horror, excitement and sheer annoyance. He hated it when things like this happened, there was a good chance this person will never be identified and the amount of work involved was unbelievable. He would much rather find the killer of modern day murders, at least that way there is a much larger chance of finding the killer alive and justice might well be done. Jake ordered a tent to be put up, pronto! The rain was really coming down and though there was no way of knowing yet how long this body had been there, the less contamination the better; this case was messed up enough without adding to the problems. In all honesty, Jake was convinced that Simon was barking up the wrong tree; this case didn't need the police. . .it needed a blumin' miracle.

~#~

Carson

Simon opened the entrance door for the police station. Collette walked in first, followed by Carson, then finally Simon let go of the door and stepped through too. The first person Carson noticed was his mother; her dark brown eyes matched her skin perfectly, but they didn't look very happy, Carson knew what was coming. Wesley, Carson's younger brother, by fifteen months was sat with her, he was smirking, with the 'you're in trouble,' look in his eyes.

"Sit with your mother, we'll call you in a minute, just need to sort something out first; Mrs Jones, sorry if this is an inconvenience for you but we must get to the bottom of this." Collette said, hoping that all would be well with Carson.

"Can I ask what all of this is about, the police officer that came to see me was very vague; is Carson in any kind of trouble?"

"No, well, not that we know of at this moment, Carson is the primary witness to a very brutal murder, we need nothing more than a statement from him."

Mrs Jones raised her eyebrows and gave a very prolonged nod, as if to say, 'well, if it is a must.'

"We can't really discuss too much here, we will fill you in better when we have an interview room set up."

Mrs Jones merely pursed her lips and though she didn't want to show it in front of her two very young and naive children, a flash of deep worry spread across her face as the thought suddenly dawned on her. 'If my child is witness to a murder, will that put us in any kind of danger?' She knew the kids around these parts and did everything within her power to keep her children safe from the gangs and the drugs that she knew freely flowed on the streets after dark. She knew her children thought she was very strict and sometimes downright mean and spiteful, but she did it, not for her own sake, but because she loved her children enough to know that being a parent is not a popularity contest, she had to keep them safe no matter what. Carson leaned in and put in head on his mothers shoulder. She patted the side of his face tenderly; she knew that Carson must have seen something so horrible; she knew that he must be scared.

Mrs Jones and the boys were not waiting for very long and not a word was said in the waiting room between them as they sat anticipating the return of one of the officers.

The interview room was a dull grey colour; the walls were magnolia and had the odd bit of coffee or tea stain here and there. Mrs Jones thought that the light strips on the ceiling were too bright and would cause her to have a headache if she spent too much time under them. There was a small table in the corner. Five wooden chairs, not one of them very comfortable looking, in fact, Mrs Jones would've described the room as being shabby and a poor excuse of where her taxes go.

"Sorry about the lack of space, there's a lot going on tonight and we just don't have any other rooms available."

"Let's just get this over and done with shall we, my children will need their supper soon and time's getting on." Mrs Jones sighed.

The police officers informed Mrs Jones about everything they could share with her, the reason why Carson was there, what he claimed he'd seen and Carson defended himself, pleading with them that what he'd seen was the truth. Deep down he knew that he would not be believed; all his efforts would turn out to be in vane, let's face it, how many people are really going to believe that a person can just burst into flames for no sensible reason?

"Was there anything at all that may make any sense, did she say anything before she died, was you really there at all or are you just making the whole damn thing up?"

Carson looked up to his mother and then to Simon. "There was one thing. . .she said something, it sounded like Henry Schnieber or sheeber or something like that."

"A name?"

“Huh huh.” Carson nodded.

Simon gave the name to Collette to work on, “find out just who this Henry Schnieber or whatever his name is.”

~#~

Just then, in the foyer a tall, white male with fair hair, in a striped blue and white zip up jacket came in. He’d got a double cheese burger in one hand and a milkshake of some sort in the other.

The half brazen woman sitting in an almost perfect uniform asked him what she could do for him.

He laughed and the female officer swore there was more than milkshake in that cardboard cup, “You’re looking for the murderer of that daft woman in the park aint ya?”

A pause.

“Well, you ain’t gonna find anything sitting there. You need to look back sixty odd years ago, me granddad told me about this sort of thing happenin’ in the war, he was the copper on the case,” the man narrowed his eyes, “they just put it all down to war crimes. . .nuffin’ ever come of it. . .funny how it’s happenin’ again ain't it?”

Before the female police officer could stop him or say anything, he had gone out of the police station. She ran to the exit door, tried to call him back, but he’d gone. . .where though? she couldn’t see. Thank goodness they got CCTV footage of what he’d just said. She wrote down everything that has just happened and walked into the interview room where Collette and Simon were still talking to Carson and Mrs Jones. Wesley sat in the corner not saying anything, drinking the weak hot chocolate that Simon had got for him out of the vending machine the same time as he got Mrs Jones and Carson a cup of tea.

~#~

Collette

Collette left the interview room immediately and researched the name Henry Schnieber, along with the old case that the mad man in the foyer was referring to. What she'd found sent her a pale white, she found cases like this going back to 1856. The pictures were graphic and terribly similar to what they had found in the park. She'd be terribly surprised if there were not more remains about Greeley like the ones found on the side of the Canal. She knew they needed help, not the kind of help any police officer can give; she needed an investigative medium. She was starting to believe the boys story, as strange as it all seemed, it was all starting to come together. The name Henry Schnieber, was according to what she'd found, a rather popular one.

She'd found an old missing persons report from the 1850's, her heart almost jumped to her mouth when the first person on the list was Henry himself.

Greeley's Missing Persons Reports (1856)

Name: Henry Watts Schnieber
Age: 42
Height: Unknown
Weight: Unknown
Description: Italian, English speaking, short dark hair.
Has not been seen for five days; friends are concerned if seen please report to Greeley Police Station. Not popular with town's folk, no one is reported to have seen him in the last 24 hours.

Name: Anthony Wilts
Age: 33
Height: 5 foot 7 inches
Weight: Around 13 stone
Description: English speaking. Blonde hair, short back and sides. Moustache. Known to wear a bowler hat at all times.
Last seen five days ago in Greeley Town Centre. No reports of any sighting since. Please report to Greeley Police Station if seen.

Name: Derrick Sanders
Age: 39
Height: Unknown

Weight: Around 14 Stone
Description: Heavily built man with dark, narrow eyes. Short Dark hair, Moustache. Last seen five days ago in Greeley Town Centre. No reports of any sighting in the last 24 hours...

And the list went on. The thing that stunned Collette more than the reports themselves were the fact that no matter how much she looked, she couldn't find anything to suggest that these reports had been followed up. There was nothing else on these missing persons not even reports to say that they had been found; nothing, it made her wonder what type of people these were to have no one care enough about them to check on them, not even the police, there was no search, not a thing. Just, what had they done to just disappear like that?

Collette decided she was going to see Jake before she went back to Simon; she needed to know what was actually found at the canal site. She was sure that Simon was still busy anyway.

~#~

Jake

There were three skeletons found on the canal side, not just one, and though nothing could be proven right now, Jake had got it into his head that the police might be looking for an ancient serial killer. Jake and his team of forensics scoured the place from top to bottom; he was convinced there wouldn't be any concrete evidence to suggest his theory. Though he was excited about the small cloth bag that had been found under the excavated charred bones, it contained a letter, a gold ring and several keys bunched up together in a tight knotted string loop. All the keys looked aged to the point where they would've only fit a very old lock, and they were red with rust. The letter was almost falling apart to the touch, but it could hold a very important clue on as to whom these people were.

'Nah, that would be too easy,' Jake thought to himself. 'Nevertheless that letter is going to be restored'.

~#~

Carrie Anne

It wasn't long after that that the letter was given to a member of staff in the lab to uncover what was said in it. The lab tech. almost shed a tear at the sheer beauty of the words; having been single for far too long, she wished with all her heart that she could find someone with such a sensitive heart, but she thought that people like that don't exist anymore. The letter was written in Italian, but as Carrie Anne was fluent in the language; she easily translated it to English.

To My Darling Audrina,

How are you my love, I nearly have enough saved up to come to be with you, are you okay my darling? Please write back as soon as you can to let me know. Every day I go crazy thinking about you and missing you in my heart, I can still smell the sweet scent of your hair. I am saving up and doing my work here as fast as I can so I can return to you my love.

When you are sad and missing me, just remember that I love you and how beautiful you are. When we are together next, I am going to ask your father for your hand in marriage. I am counting the seconds and I cherish the day that I can see your beautiful smiling face again.

I will see you soon my darling, send my regards to your family.

Love you forever.

H

"Henry!"

"Oh, for goodness sake you just scared the life out of me."

"Sorry, made you jump?" asked Collette with an amused look on her face.

Carrie Anne Barlow had got a lot of things on her mind, she had broke up with her girlfriend about two years ago and though it took her a while to get over her, she was ready go out and try to open new doors for herself. At the age of twenty six she was still scared to tell her parent's that she's gay. She knows how they'd react, pretty much the same way her ex-girlfriend's parent's reacted when she came out the closet a few years ago, they disowned her, completely washed their hands off of her. Collette knew about Carrie Anne's predicament; she and Carrie Anne were very good friends, when either one had the time, they would spend time together, as friends do and talk about the same things all women do across the continents; relationships, make-up, nails, work and their home life. Carrie Anne was scared to tell her parent's because she didn't want to be judged for something that she couldn't help being. . .gay.

"What makes you say Henry?"

Collette showed Carrie Anne everything that she had gathered on this Henry person. Carrie Anne translated the letter to her and the expression on Collette's face was one of total confusion; this letter, compared to the information she'd found on Henry, just didn't fit this persona.

"It just goes to show doesn't it, about judging books and covers." Collette muttered.

Carrie Anne nodded slightly, "yeah." She said with a slight giggle in her voice.

"Have you taken these to Simon yet? He'll want to know about them."

Gently nodding, "I know, no though not yet, I needed to know what was in that letter first, and I gotta tell ya, this really doesn't sound like the same person."

Carrie Anne smiled, "perhaps he had a multiple personality dis-order, or maybe he was just in love, people do crazy things for love."

Collette pursed her lips, "Tis true."

~#~

Collette

Carrie Anne continued with working on the letter, trying to preserve it as best as she could. Meanwhile. . .Collette made her way over to Simon's office.

"Find anything?" Simon asked feeling a little at a loss.

Collette gave a broad smile and a knowing look; she raised her eyebrows and sat down on the semi-comfortable chair reserved mainly for co-workers, clients, victims and criminals; Simon sat on what Collette called the power chair behind the desk. She gave him everything that she had got, but to Simon none of it made much sense.

"This is all very good, but what has this 19th century murder got to do with everything that we have found today?"

There was no way she was going to let Simon get the better of her on this one, her theory was right and she knew it, her gut told her so. She cocked her head slightly to the right and narrowed her eyes. "Have you had the carbon dating reports off those bodies yet?"

"Don't answer a question with a question; what's the connection?" Simon was tired, and it was showing, he sat with his elbows on the desk, his fingertips covering his mouth while his chin rested on his thumbs.

Collette knew that he wasn't going to buy this, he was so sceptical about everything; he didn't even believe in God, which in Collette eyes was a sacrilege by itself. She knew it wasn't her place to judge, but she couldn't help secretly doing so, after all she is a DI, a woman and though others didn't always think so, just as human as everyone else.

"I think we need to bring in an investigative medium, I think this is a paranormal case, and I don't think we have any business being in it."

Simon's face changed from annoyance to amused and back to being annoyed again in the space of 10 seconds, then he just burst out laughing.

~#~

Jake

Jake had spent all day in the laboratory, he had had those bones carbon dated and he was not surprised when the results came back as 160 years old. It wasn't long before he had started the artist profile of how these people would've looked. This was the thing that took the time. He didn't hate this part of the job, he was fully qualified and very talented, but he really felt like he was wasting his time, even if he could find out who these people were and one of them turned out the be a killer in the 19th century. How on earth can that solve anything, it has nothing to do with the killing of recent victims? He was so frustrated.

~#~

Collette

'Who was it that said being honest was the best policy?' Collette thought as she left the office of the still laughing Simon; he thought that bringing someone in that pretends to be able to see into things 'supernaturally' was a really bad idea and should never have been thought of in the first place. Collette was really quite hurt from his reaction, she had told him everything she could, showed him everything she had found, and though in her mind's eye everything was pointing to something that needed some spiritual help, to Simon the idea was so preposterous that he couldn't help but laugh.

Collette went to the canteen to try and think over a cup of half decent tea, she never drank coffee at work, or anywhere else for that matter unless it was one she had made herself, with coffee she was unbelievably fussy, if there was just one grain out of place, it made the entire cup taste like toxic waste to her.

~#~

Simon

In the meantime, Simon was in his office, pondering over what had been said, thinking about the possibilities, then again he dismissed it, no way, it's not possible. He went over and over the work she had found; the actual likely-hood of it being Spontaneous Human Combustion; again he looked at the newspaper report that was now on his desk. The boy, Carson said that he had heard June say something along the lines of 'Henry Schnieber.'

Simon grabbed his coat and went back to the crime scene, maybe they had been looking at this whole thing from the wrong direction after all, no matter how absurd the idea, he had to check out all angles, that was his job and his duty.

Simon honestly didn't know what he was looking for when he got to the part of the park where June had died. He was under the impression that the forensics team was on top of it all and in all honesty, he felt a like he was going slightly mad. What on earth was he doing there? Then something stopped him in his tracks and his train of thought, there was something, a black gooey liquid type thing that was hanging off the tree right next to where June had died, she was so close to this particular tree that the bottom of the trunk was slightly burnt. He pulled out a small plastic bag out of his inside pocket, at the same time he pulled out his black pen that his sister had bought him for his birthday; he didn't want to ruin it, but there really wasn't anything else that he could use without risking violating the goo any more than it was already violated, he had to get it to the lab.

The rain had come down pretty hard earlier; he was rather surprised that this stuff hadn't been washed away, but that was just a passing thought. He pulled a face as if it was some kind of excrement, it was rather nasty.

The day was getting on and the night was starting to draw in; twilight was upon him and the sun was going down at an alarming rate for this time of year. He ran back to the car and brought out the torch he had cooped up in the boot of his saloon, he switched it on and instantly in the dark shone a beam of light. He went back to the scene of the crime and continued to look for anything else that might not be of the norm for an area like this, any kind of evidence, was evidence and he now knew that there were things in this world that just could not be explained, like that terrible blackish coloured goo. Secretly deep down he thought that he would never be able to find anything else in this place.

So he was surprised with what happened next.

The light in his torch started to flicker, until the thing just went dead, he bashed the head of the torch with the side his hand in the hope that it would come back on, but nothing. "Darn torch, these batteries were new the other day as well," he thought out loud. Frustrated with the situation he threw the torch on the ground; it bounced lightly as the soft grass took the brunt of its fall.

To the left of where he was standing he was horrified to hear the sound of horses coming around the corner; he could swear he could hear the sound of a carriage as well, he heard the sound of the reins as they tapped lightly against the horses backs. Simon was scared of horses; he had been since he was twenty three as he was chased by one. He had only been stroking one on the side of the canal but the horse decided he didn't want to be stroked. He didn't hate horses, not by a long shot, but his fear gave him a respect for them that made him keep his distance. After all, behind those hooves, there is a fair bit of muscle, they could seriously injure a person with one good swift kick in the right place and goodness knows what could happen if they rear up. Simon's heart started to beat a little faster than usual, even with those horses, the carriage just sounded unusual, things like that rarely exist these days, there is no need for them not in this day and age. He knew that he should stop the driver and ask what they are doing out here at this time of night in the park, but fear got the better of him and though he felt like a coward he decided the best thing he could do is hide behind the tree, that idea sounded really quite pathetic to him but it was the best he could do to keep out of sight and still be able to get a good look at those horses.

As the horses came around the corner in view of Simon, Simon noticed that the solidity of the horses and the coach was questionable. They were almost ghost like, even the jangle of the reins seemed distant even though they were right there practically in front of him. It freaked him out that there was no driver, well there was a driver, the horses, all four of them, were being driven, but he was not visible. Simon's eyes opened wide, his mouth and throat suddenly became dry, and his heart seemed to beat ten times faster. He thought for a short while that it might just be his mind playing tricks on him, it clearly wasn't. Simon knew he wasn't going mad, he knew what he could see was real. He suddenly became aware that his back was not protected, he felt like in order to stay safe he needed eyes on the back of his head too. Though the coach was only passing by, taking just a matter of seconds, it seemed to take a very long time for it to pass. No sooner the ghostly coach had gone out of sight, the torch that Simon had thrown to the ground flickered on again. Simon picked it up, ran to his car, started the engine and drove off, he didn't look back and he swore that was the last time he would find himself in that park again, on his own, after dark.

Simon pulled up outside the entrance to the lab. His heart still felt like it was going nineteen to the dozen and he still felt paranoid that he wasn't on his own. He wanted to get out of the car and into the lab as fast as possible, but he found that his legs were like jelly and he couldn't get up just yet if he tried. He knew the moment he tried he'd be on the ground, trying to pull himself out of a helpless situation. So he just sat there for a few minutes, rested his forehead on the steering wheel and cried. Simon didn't really know what he was crying for and being a grown man he certainly didn't want anyone to see him pouring his heart out to the dashboard, but he found that once he started crying, he just couldn't stop. He was so upset about something and for the love of God he just didn't know what. He knew though that he needed to get this black goo in the lab before Jake came out to close up for the night. He forced himself out of the car and held on to the door handle for his dear life; he stood there a few minutes just to steady himself. When he felt sure that he would be okay, he let go and walked through the rotating doors, through the foyer and over to the lift; he waited silently...

~#~

Collette

Collette decided to make her way home; she knew there was no point in talking to Simon while he was in this mood, he was impossible to talk to; something was niggling at her though, something just didn't feel right. It was almost as if she was having this sixth sense that something was wrong. She turned her car around and started to make her way back to lab, if it was closed then it was closed; she knew she wouldn't be able to sleep tonight without at least checking.

When Collette got to the building all the main lights were still on, the swivel doors were still turning. It was getting on for ten o'clock and normally this time of night everyone would've gone home. At least that is what she thought Jake was going to be doing; he said that he wouldn't be too far behind her when she walked out the door to get her belongings from his office.

Collette walked through the foyer and headed towards the same lift that Simon headed to not twenty minutes ago. She found him on the floor, looking slightly disorientated. Collette ran to his aide, it looked like he had just fell from where he stood, just collapsed to the ground in a heap, it didn't look like there were any serious injuries, but Simon sat up holding his forehead. Collette gave him a tissue from her handbag to mop up the tiny bit of blood that was visible from the wound caused by hitting his head on the ground as he fell.

"I really think you should let me take you to the hospital, even if it is just to let them check you over." Collette made it quite clear that she was concerned that Simon was hurt, I mean after all, how many people collapse for no reason?

"No. I'm fine." Simon gave Collette a thankful smile, "honestly, don't worry. I have had a bit of a weird night; I think it may have just caught up with me, that's all."

Simon told her of the park and the ghostly coach, he wasn't even worried that she wouldn't believe him, after all it was her idea to bring in a medium, it was obvious to him that she didn't need convincing of the truth.

"Did you hit your head a bit too hard?" Collette asked with humour in her voice.

Simon frowned, he was sure she'd believe him.

"Don't worry, I believe you," Collette said, almost as if she could read his mind.

For now, Simon was content with Collette's answer.

~#~

Simon

Simon worked through these last few months in a bit of a daze. He couldn't stop thinking about that damn coach he had seen in the park. He knew it was not a figment of his imagination, but a figment of his imagination was the only way that he could explain what he saw; he was a sceptic, more than a sceptic, he just did not believe and he didn't want to believe. Believing in something like that meant there was some kind of life after death and being a copper with an aptitude for all things science, meant that if what he saw was real, then that would screw up his whole atheist belief system; Simon was confused to say the least.

Though three months is a relatively long time in a murder case, neither Collette nor Simon was getting any closer to finding out who did this. They were both eager for Jake to finish his artistic profile of one of the skeletons they found on the bank of the canal. There was an air of excitement about the place when Simon got the call off Jake to say that the profile was nearly finished and they could come to the lab anytime to take the necessary pictures or whatever it was that the police needed with it now.

The whole case was getting excruciatingly confusing; the DCI wanted answers and he was not expecting the case to go the way it was. He slammed the report down on his desk and shrieked.

"For crying out loud, I asked you to find the killer, not frolic about with ghouls and ghosts, or whatever it is you would have me call 'em." DCI Mason said, tormented by what seems to be a total waste of police time.

Simon was equally as frustrated, both with the case and the DCI.

"If I remember correctly, Sir, it was you that put me on this case in the first place, you wanted me to go and check out these Spontaneous Human Combustion (SHC) cases and that is exactly what I am doing. What would you prefer, for me to bring in some innocents off the street and frame them for the murders, just because you want the case to make sense? Well I can't do that Sir. You know yourself that every case takes its own form, and this is just the form this one is taking. There is no rational explanation for it; it just looks to me like you were right after all.

"In the case of June, the lady who was killed in the park, it doesn't look like it was SHC, she wasn't killed by any living person nor was it suicide, there is a killer on the loose Sir, but not one of this world."

DCI Mason could not believe what he was hearing, he shook his head.

"I think you need a break; I'm taking you off the case." The DCI shrugged, "I don't know. Go on holiday for a couple of weeks. Soak up some sun. I'm putting Amory and Wells on it. There is a living person responsible for Junes death and I'm damn well gonna find out who it is; now get out of my office before I call a damn psychiatrist!"

Simon almost lost his temper, he went red in the face but calmed down instantly when DCI Mason looked at him as if to say, 'carry on, you'll lose your job.'

"No! You can't take me off this case, what about Collette and Jake; their findings are just the same as mine. I am not giving up on this case Sir, paid or unpaid, I am going to get to the bottom of it, you're just going to end up arresting the wrong person."

"And what d'you suggest I tell the papers' that a ghost is going around killing people? The world is going to think that we're insane."

"So this is what it all boils down to, the press and what people think of you, you don't want to be a laughing stock so you're willing to throw me off the case to condemn some poor soul, just so you don't have to look bad; what kind of police officer are you?"

"You are swimming in unchartered waters Simon be careful how you choose your next words, they may well be your last in this office." The DCI said, infuriated.

Simon bent down to look DCI Mason in the eyes, "do as you will, but this case is mine." Simon stands up and walks out the door, slamming it hard enough for the glass to rattle in its frame. He takes in a deep breath and moves on.

DCI Mason looked slightly bewildered; shaking his head he calls his secretary from the intercom on his desk to get Amory and Wells in his office, pronto!

~#~

Jake

Jake's eyes were tired, they appeared to have bags under them, and he had practically worked day and night to get this profile done; he didn't really want to stay on this case and the sooner he had it finished the better. The feel of the whole thing just made him feel dark, dreary and uncomfortable. It didn't help that the little bit of sleep he was getting was being disturbed by some unknown voice in his head constantly repeating like a record stuck on a turn table. . . "Finish this and leave. . . finish this and leave." It was driving him mad, he had visions of a fire, an old cobbled street, one that he knew, and he knew he knew but he couldn't put his finger on it, and that made him feel extremely uncertain. Why he felt like this, to Jake, it was a mystery.

~#~

Simon

The day was rather hot and the sun was powerfully shining through the windscreen, both the passenger and driver windows were down as Simon pulled into the car park of the lab. He was still smouldering over the DCI's words in his office; he'd told Collette everything that had been said but since then Collette had had her own run in with the DCI. He had taken her off the case too, but like Simon, she was not going to give up on this case either.

~#~

Collette

As they both stepped out of the car, Collette pulled her handbag over her shoulder. She didn't particularly want to leave it in the car because Simon was keeping his sunroof half open to try to stop the car from feeling like an oven when they get back into it. She didn't feel safe leaving it there, in full view for anyone to reach down and take.

Collette hoped with all her heart that the profile had not only been finished, but the photos taken for police files had already been done; she had someone in mind to go and visit later and it was important that Simon and the photos were available to go with her.
"She is quite old, and very fragile, both mentally and physically, but I am certain that with these photos, my grandmother will be able to help us with our investigations."

Simon raised an eyebrow; he wasn't convinced, he knew that Collette's Grandmother had been locked up in that home for nearly 30 years; she was convinced that someone was out to kill her, that whoever it was, was back and there was nothing that could protect her once he knew where she was. She put herself in that home and she never, ever stepped out of it, not once in all that time.

Luckily, everything was ready in the lab. neither Simon nor Collette had to wait too long for the photos. Collette was a little bit worried about Jake and the way he has gone from his normal, eager self to this almost shell of a man, something wasn't right with him, instead of the thirty something man that he was, he was acting like he was in his seventies, he looked drawn and old. Collette thought that this job was really getting to him more than he would want to let on to anyone, though to her, it was obvious something was wrong.

~#~

Simon

Simon and Collette pulled up outside St. Francis home for mental health. The sky was blue with a few of those small white fluffy clouds scattered here and there. The building itself reminded Simon of a large, white castle. The entrance had a huge bay window and a few wide shallow steps that led to the inner door towards the foyer. Inside the foyer was a huge grand staircase. It looked odd being in this building, not because of the look of the building, but because one normally associates staircases like this in museums, mansions or film sets. Simon had even seen one in a college once, but never in a home for the mentally ill, not until now. The home was spacious; the staircase was a white marble and with the natural light that came into the building from those big, wide lead windows it made the whole place look too clinical to him.

This was not the first time Simon had stepped into this building, but the bright awe and clinical energy of the place never ceased to amaze him. The chandelier on the ceiling sparkled causing rainbows on the wall through the prisms of the crystal cut glass. It was very beautiful. In the time it took Simon to look around, Collette had already been to the reception desk and asked which room her grandmother was in. Some of the patients are moved from one room to another, solely just for a change of scenery on a regular basis, depending on their illness.

Both Simon and Collette were shown up the grand staircase and then through a few corridors. Simon and Collette were politely ushered into the room where the lady they came to see was sitting on a wheelchair in front of a rather large and bright window.

“Gran?” Collette asked, rather cautiously.

Collette’s gran turned around in her chair to face them; for her age she still had a natural beauty. One could tell that when she was young she would have been a stunner. Her hair was long and grey and rested nicely on her shoulders. Simon thought rather collectively that this lady didn’t look like she needed to be in a place like this; she appeared rather well put together and didn't seem in any way unwell.

"Gran, this is DI Jackson." Collette wasn't sure whether to go formal or stay casual when introducing people to him. "DI Jackson, this is my gran, Josephine Hadley."

Josephine Hadley, where did he hear that name before? Then the penny dropped...of course. "You're the lady who was found in the. . ."

"Nature reserve?" She smiled sadly, "yes, don't tell me, you think I'm crazy too."

Simon was just about to disagree but couldn't get his words out in time.

"Don't worry Mr Jackson, most people do, I'm used to it."

Simon would've protested further but Collette gave him a 'not to' look. "Please call me Simon."

"Fine, well that is the end of the formalities then Simon I am afraid you're just going to have to call me Josie." Then she smiled a smile that would have once lit up a very dark room indeed, and Simon knew the ice had been broken.

"I gave you my grans file the same time as I gave you the file on the other SHC (Spontaneous Human Combustion) reports from the nineteen forties. There were no explanations to the deaths of these people and my gran is the only survivor, but no one believed her when she told the truth. So they put her in an old asylum and put the deaths down to war crimes."

"Hold on a minutes ere, whose telling the story, me or you, if you, then why are you here?"

Collette smiled, Josephine had got a point.

"Were there any burn marks on your body when you were found?" Simon asked Josephine, trying not to look at Collette; he didn't want to offend her, she looked like she knew how to handle herself and didn't really want to get on the wrong side of her.

"No, but my hair turned instantly grey and I lost the ability to speak for a while; when I did eventually open my mouth, no sane person on Gods earth would have believed what I told 'em."

"You told them about the ghost coach?"

"Huh huh." Josie nodded in agreement.

Simon scratched the side of his jaw and rubbed his cheek with the palm of his hand. He closed his eyes tight for just a couple of seconds and memorized the coach in which she referred to.

"You've seen it, haven't you?" It wasn't a question, more like a statement of knowledge.

Reluctantly, Simon nodded.

Josie smiled, "things will change for you now, you know. No one actually really lives after they have seen that thing. I might be a living, breathing human being, but apart from the day I met Collette's grandfather and the day my daughter and grandchildren was born I can honestly say that I have hardly lived a single day of my life. I've existed, survived. That coach will leave a curse on your soul, one that will not allow you to move on till the day you depart from this earth, even then, you will be bound to stay, until the day his soul can be put to rest, and that can't happen unless. . ."

A short pause

"Unless what, Josie; what is it?"

"Unless his soul can be united with Audrina's; they need to find each other, otherwise, he will not rest, and neither will you, I, nor any of the other souls he has tortured."

Simon swallowed hard. Every hair on his body stood up on end, he really didn't believe in curses, but then he really didn't believe in spirits either until about a couple of months ago.

"Curses only have power if you believe in them." Simon said quietly.

Josie smiled slightly, and gave a small and light nod. She settled in her chair.

"Find Audrina's soul Simon and you will lift this curse. Do it while you are still young. It is she, he is looking for, he will not stop killing until you find her and your life will not be your own until you solve this case. Do not rely on the police to sort this out; they haven't got a clue where to start looking. Now go, I'm tired, I need to sleep." Josie gestured towards to door.

Collette bent down to give her a kiss on the forehead and whispered 'thank you,' in her ear.

Josie gave one careful nod and fell to sleep almost instantly in her chair.

Simon was not sorry to be leaving the old building and if he was being true to himself, what Josie had just been talking about really shook him up, curses!? No way, how could he believe in such things? People make their own way in life; they work hard and do good things and good things will happen, do bad things and bad things will happen. That was his way of thinking and there was no changing that, but then, if that was true, then why did he have this terrible feeling, this weight on his shoulders that had been there since the night he saw that coach. What was that, and the curse? Nothing made sense to him anymore, but then, he wondered if it was supposed to. His whole belief system was changing; it was devastating his life, because even though he wanted to, almost needed to believe in something, he just didn't know what to believe in. Simon's faith in everything, even his atheism had gone. He felt well and truly lost. Maybe that was his curse.

The car beeped as the alarm system deactivated. Simon got into the driver's side and Collette followed suit at the passenger side. He didn't look at her, not even as much as a glance; he started the car and drove. He didn't really know where he was going and Collette understood enough to not get freaked out by his lack of concentration, but enough was enough. Collette was not going to be lost in middle of nowhere because Simon wasn't holding it together very well.

"Stop the car! Let me drive." Collette's tone held no prisoner's and Simon knew it; he stopped the car just as she'd asked. He pulled over near a grass verge, there didn't seem to be anything for miles. It really would've been a very nice area to visit if the circumstances had been different. No sooner the car had stopped, he cried; this time he knew exactly what he was crying for, deep down, no matter how much he wanted to deny it, Josie, was right. But how on earth did she know? He looked straight at Collette, come to think of it; there really was something haunting about Josie. Did Collette know what that was?

"Penny dropped?" Collette remarked, raising an eyebrow.

Simon frowned, "how did she know about the curse?"

"She has lived her own curse, which is why she is who she is."

"Who is she?"

"She is Josephine Hadley, wife, mother, sister, daughter, grandmother and Psychic. She can't call for the dead; otherwise she would've ended her own curse a long time ago. She can normally pick up on the path a person is already walking; she tells their past, not their future, but every now and then she'll have a premonition of their future, but different people's futures change with their circumstances. She can sense other people's feelings, she knows when there is something wrong, and generally she is spot on every single time. She knew you saw the coach because she could sense it from you."

"Has she always been like this?" Simon urged.

"Only since her own encounter with the coach, my gran has been forced to live a life of torment, her gifts are her curse. She has no pleasure from them and they are nothing but a burden to her. She is surrounded by the knowledge of her own fate and that scares the life out of her, but the truth is, she lives in fear and living in fear is a terrible thing."

Simon felt so sorry for Collette's whole family, and of course for Josephine, but he was just as confused as he ever was.

“I think we should do your suggestion and bring in a psychic investigator, we need to try and break this curse.”

Collette raised an eyebrow, the same thing concerned her the last time she thought about this. Would there be anyone interested in taking this curse on? She thought she knew the answer. Every time her gran had thought up this relatively good idea, there just wasn’t anyone willing to put themselves in this line of fire, it was dangerous, very dangerous, if it went wrong the house or person/s wouldn’t only be left with an unwanted spirit; but there would most likely be deaths too. No one in her family had ever been willing to put anyone else in danger, and her gran, who constantly had a bad feeling about it, would just not let that happen, disturbed or not, Josie’s a good woman. Collette put her concerns to Simon.

“But it was your idea in the first place; why on earth would you come up with the idea if you’re just going to mill all over it now?”

“There are some people out there that are willing to do it, but it’s finding them, and then it’s getting my gran to come along. I don’t know what she is more scared of, the thought of doing séance or the thought of coming face to face with the spirit that put the curse on her in the first place.”

“Well, you can’t blame her for that, can you? I mean c’mon, she is just going to need a little bit of reassurance. She’ll be fine in the end and so will I. I am sure of it, we all will be.

Simon felt compelled to tell the DCI how they were getting on now they had a new lead, but he quickly realised how pointless that would be. The DCI wouldn’t listen to them anyway, as far as the DCI was concerned, Simon and Collette were deluded and off the case.

Simon and Collette had eventually found a medium that was willing to help. She was an eccentric young woman who reminded him a little bit of a woman he had seen on TV a while ago. Simon recalls the telephone conversation that they had and her voice, it sounded almost like she’s a little bit highty tighty, but at the same time as common as muck. He couldn’t figure her out. He shrugged; it didn’t matter to him what she sounded like as long as she does her job and does it well. Simon called Collette and made arrangements with her to meet Pamela and take her to their preferred hotel. Collette now had the job of informing her gran and with a lot of persuasion, Josie was willing to join. The only thing they needed now was the letter that was found in the bag buried under the bodies. So his next port of call was Jake's lab.

~#~

Jake

Jake seemed like he had been run ragged with these bones that had been found, it wasn't just one, or two skeletons, but he had to put a face to three of them. His laboratory had practically been turned into an office come art studio. It was driving him crazy and he didn't know why. He knew that if he kept working like this he would run himself down into the ground, but there was nothing he could do about it and he still had those voices in his head. . . 'Finish this and leave, finish this and leave.' He had to finish, it was almost like something had possessed him, and he just couldn't stop working, not until he could finish this and leave.

Jakes friends and colleagues had seen this change in him and were extremely worried; they tried to tell him to stop and take a break but the only comments they got back off him was, 'I'll break your neck if you tell me to take a break one more time.' Jake didn't like the person he was becoming, it wasn't like him to be violent or nasty to people and the people who worked with him everyday knew that. He's a good, honest, hard working man with skills and talents that most people would kill for. They knew that something was wrong, but they didn't know what or how to help him. They'd noticed his nose bleeds and they could only put it down to stress. Security had even escorted him off the premises to get some rest; but Jake was not willing to go, so each time he found his way back in, he couldn't go, not until he was finished.

~#~

Simon

Simon had the second shock of his life when he walked into Jakes lab. He had never seen Jake so uptight and wound up. Simon walked into the laboratory with just one thing on his mind, that letter and if he could take it the key too. Maybe that key had a significant part to play in Henry's curse, but when he saw how Jake was reacting, it worried him.

“Jake, you don’t look so good mate; you need to take a break.”

Jake looks up from his work, his eyes are murderous.

“What d’you want?” He snarled.

Simon had never heard him talk like that before and the sharpness of his voice startled him.

“I need the letter and the keys that were found with those bodies.”

“What? No!”

“What d’you mean ‘no,’ I need them I have to have them; it’s to assist with the case.”

“What case? You’ve been kicked off it, remember!”

Simon obviously did remember, but regardless he made his way over to the cupboard in which he knew that the evidence was held. He took no notice of what Jake was saying because Jake was suffering from sleep deprivation. Just as he got there he stopped dead, scared to move either to the left or to the right. He found it within himself to move and look at Jake with fear and questioning eyes. On the wall next to where Simon was standing a carving knife was wobbling from side to side as its blade was edged into the plasterboard.

Jake stood there, breathing heavy. “I SAID NO!” Jake shouted. “They are not leaving this lab, they belong with these bodies. They cannot be moved!”

Simon’s heart beat nineteen to the dozen, anger was not the only emotion he was feeling, it was more than that, anger, fear and confusion. Jake was his friend, not once in the ten years he had known him had he ever acted in such a way. He knew that it must have been the bones of Henry Schnieber that was doing this to him. It must have been there was no other explanation. He knew one thing, and that was he had to get Jake out of this lab, and away from those bones, if he didn’t, they would end up either killing him, or Jake would end up killing someone else. Simon knew he would have to take him forcefully; there was no way he was going to go willingly.

"Jake Milford, I am arresting you for the attempted murder of a police officer. You don't have to say anything, but what you do say may be used against you in a court of law."

"No, no, no, no, no...No!"

Jake struggled and gasped for air, panic set in and breathing became a problem. It was almost like he knew that if he left the room something on the other side of the door was going to get him. In the weeks that Jake had lived and breathed in the same air of that lab, the walls had almost shrouded him like a cloak, and just like a child being taken away from his security blanket, Jake cried, of both fear and uncertainty. Simon practically had to drag him out of that room, and with anyone else he would have called for backup and really locked them up. But Simon knew what was happening to Jake and why. He had absolutely no proof that the profile Jake was working on was indeed Henry Schnieber but he just knew, he didn't know how he knew, he just did and it was those bones that were causing all the trouble.

Jake protested and cried and tried to tell Simon that he was condemning him to death by not allowing him to finish the profiles before he could go. For some reason Henry wanted those profiles to be finished before he could leave, the consequences were going to be terrible. He needed to get back into that laboratory before it was too late.

~#~

Collette

Collette had spoken to the medium over the phone since Simon had spoken to her and she was on her way to pick the medium up from the train station, but first she had to pick up her gran from the home.

There was only one destination left after that and that was to the hotel room Simon and Collette had booked to perform the séance that would either make or break the case. She hoped with all her heart that this medium, Pamela Heart, will be successful in what they need to do; goodness knows that would happen if it went wrong. Collette, though probably the strongest out of the group barring Pamela, was scared, she wished that she didn't have to do this. It just didn't feel right. But she had to, for the sake of the people of Greeley, her family and her friends.

This wasn't about her or her feelings, she had to put her personal thoughts away and be strong, it was imperative.

~#~

Simon

The Sanderson's Hotel sign was lit up in the middle of the day. Simon couldn't see the point to it, and it was just a waste of electricity to him. Jake sat in the passenger seat, his heartbeat had gone back to normal and he felt like a moron crying over leaving the lab, but at the same time he was still a bit freaked out that he got to feeling that way in the first place and that shook him up terribly. Simon had bought him a sweet tea from the cafe a few miles away from the laboratory and though Jake didn't really know what was going to happen at the séance, he did know that he couldn't go back to that lab any time soon. Not while those bones were still there anyway. It might be a good idea just to blow the whole damn thing up. . .problem solved.

Simon pulled up into an almost empty car park. It wasn't long before both men were heading into the foyer, neither decided to go over to the reception desk, both thought it best to wait for the ladies in the bar, that way they could go up together, it would look less weird if questions were asked.

~#~

Pamela

Pamela was worried that her train was running a little bit late. She loved the train. Well, she did when she got settled, she was claustrophobic, it always took her about ten minutes to feel comfortable, but once she had got a coffee from the little shop cabin and got used to her surroundings she was fine, enjoying watching the world go by.

Pamela had been travelling for almost three hours and, yes, she was tired but she was also relaxed, travelling always relaxed her. The countryside and all open spaces were heaven to her, and to watch it pass her by was bliss. Today she loved it more than ever. Pamela always had the attitude to live each day as if it were your last and to love life with every fibre of your being. Being a medium, it was her job and her gift to be around the dead, she hated it, to her it was not a gift, but a curse. It was morbid and she'd give anything for it to go away. So when the train approached Greeley train station she was slightly disappointed that her journey had come to an end.

Pamela had only ever spoke to Collette over the telephone; in theory there is no way she would have been able to put a face to the name, but once she got off the train and stepped on to the platform, she somehow knew to make her way to the station's little cafe. She knew she would find Collette there, but with Collette was another woman, a woman that also had abilities, a gift. It was the kind of gift that always made Pamela feel nervous to be around. She knew that Josie could pick up on her emotions from both past and present; she also knew that Josie would be able to determine what sort of person she is; silently judging her. It made her feel really uncomfortable because, it seems, her own head was the only true place she was safe, the only place that was private and she didn't want it violated. That scared her more than the thought of performing the séance they were about to contrive.

Pamela walked into the dingy cafe. The strip lights was the kind that would easily cause a headache if one had to endure it for hours and the grubby magnolia walls were scattered with fluorescent stars cut out of card that advertised specials from the menu. On the far wall was a large print of a train timetable for the platform they were on. Convenient as this place might be, it was not the sort of place a woman like Pamela would be comfortable eating it.

The first person that took Pamela's attention was the large man in the high visibility jacket standing at the counter, talking to the waitress like they had known each other for a very long time. The only other person in the cafe other than the two women that Pamela was making her way over to, was a young woman, she was obviously waiting for her train and drinking tea out of a polythene cup whilst reading a magazine of some sort. Her glasses seemed to be too far down her nose as she read the article.

Pamela's slim frame made her way over to the two women that was sitting there, looking up at her expectantly.

~#~
Josie

Initially Josie was slightly taken aback by the presence of Pamela, and just like Pamela, she needed no introduction. She knew exactly who she was the moment she stepped into the cafe. Josie took a sip of her hot tea and put the white polythene cup on the slightly stained, white granite style table. She wasn't really impressed by the persona of Pamela. Pamela was slim, pretty in a rugged way and rather toned; her long dark fringe was put up in a clip while the rest of her hair hung loose over her shoulders and stopped just above breast line. Her low cut green top showed a tattoo of a phoenix in flight.

Both Collette and Josie stood up as Pamela approached the table. They each offered a hand to shake, they introduced themselves and having got over the awkward first meeting, neither wanted to hang about and thought it would be best to head straight to Collette's car. They left the two half full cups of tea on the table for the chatty waitress to pick up.

As they exited the cafe, a high speed train raced past causing a small piece of grit to go flying into Collette's eye. She groaned and blinked a few times and tried desperately to remove the horrid pain this tiny foreign body was causing her.

"Hang on a second." Pamela muttered as she pulled out a cotton handkerchief from her Indian style cotton hand bag.

Very carefully with the corner of the handkerchief Pamela reached in and edged out the smallest piece of grit that was causing Collette so much pain. Collette didn't like anything going near her eyes, so she tried with all her might to stay still and not flinch. It was against her better judgement to allow Pamela anywhere near her eyes and by the time the grit was out, Collette's eye was slightly bloodshot and felt rather dry though she knew that it wouldn't take long for it to settle down.

"Thank you." Collette said in a bewildered manner.

Josie was grateful for that too but not impressed by Pamela's actions. She was glad her granddaughter was no longer in any pain but she didn't like people who put on airs and graces, Josie knew that was exactly what Pamela was doing.

"Just be yourself Pamela and you'll find we'll get on with each other much better if you do."

Pamela was slightly taken aback by what Josie has just said, but then she knew she was right; there was no fooling her.

~#~

Jake

Jake had just downed his third straight scotch; he needed something to calm the nerves. He didn't quite understand what had just happened and it had taken it out of him a little bit. Now he was away from the lab and those damn bones, his temperament was getting back to normal, or as normal as one can get after being stuck in the lab for seven weeks or so, convinced death will come if you leave. In all honesty though and in his defence, that is all he can remember, well, properly remember anyway, the last few weeks was rather a blur to him, like he'd just woken from a bad dream. Now his head felt like that of the world's worst hangover and the scotch was just the hair of the dog.

"At least you've got some colour back in your cheeks; I was getting a bit worried about you back there."

"In all honesty Simon, I'm confused to hell; I have no idea how it got that bad. What can I say? There is something evil about those bones. I'm sorry; I shouldn't have thrown that knife at you."

"Well, I ain't gonna lie to you Jake, it got pretty bad in there, I don't arrest my friends for no reason you know."

Jake nodded, but his attention turned to the entrance door as three women walked in; he recognised one of them as Collette but the other two he had never met before. Judging by what Simon had told him earlier, the other two must have been Josie and Pamela. He caught Pamela's eye, she smiled.

~#~
Simon

“Over night or just for the day?” The receptionist asked as she booked in the party of five to a large room in hotel.

“Just for a few hours, it’s an important business meeting.” Simon felt slightly embarrassed, he couldn’t tell the receptionist the truth, but goodness knows what kind of thoughts were going through her head as she handed over the key for room 48.

“Take the lift to the fourth floor, and it’s on your right.”

“Thank you.”

The lifts were in full view of the reception area; there were two of them, one for the odd number floors and the other for the even number floors. Simon pressed the call button for the even numbers; the doors opened instantly.

The atmosphere between the five of them was rather oppressive. Simon hated this idea, but he knew they had to do something to stop any more people being killed, more importantly, to eradicate this damn curse that loomed over their heads like a dark, thunderous cloud.

The room cost a small fortune, and as they all walked in they could see why. The floors were wooden and polished, the walls magnolia/white with the odd modern art painting. On the right was a small living area, with a flat screen LED television, a glass coffee table, and a couple of small book shelves scattered with niceties, next to that was a small, but modern writing bureau. The bathroom door was on the far left. A large double bed was situated next to it, with two bedside tables on either side, each had a lamp. Inside the top drawers of these bedside tables were, to Simon’s imagination a bible, as there is in all hotels. The ceiling was white with spot lights evenly scattered from one end of the room to the other. A round dining table stood in the middle of the room between the living and bedroom area. There was a large window with vertical blinds on the bedroom side and the same again on the living room side.

This was not something that he could put on his expenses, as neither Simon nor Collette was officially on the case anymore. So the four of them (not including Pamela as she was being paid for her time), each put their hands in their pockets and each paid equal amounts to pay for the cost of the room.

“Glad to see there is a table here, we’re missing a chair though, anyone think to bring a candle?” Pamela said as she was the first in the light airy, room. She rolled her eyes and uttered something like, ‘at least one of us remembers these things’.

“We’re paying you to remember these things.” Josie said as she heard the under breath comment.

Collette went straight for the mini bar, she didn’t care about the price, and she just wanted something there and then to calm her nerves. She had never been a part of any kind of séance or any other type of ritual for that matter and Simon in all honesty felt the same. Both had a tiny bottle of scotch, Jake opted for the gin and Josie wanted the vodka. Pamela didn’t drink, especially during the day, it gave her a headache. Before opening the gin, Jake noticed something missing and he picked up the phone receiver to rectify the problem.

“Room service? Yes, can you bring up another chair for the table please?”

Pause...

“Okay, thank you.”

It wasn’t five minutes later that there was a knock at the door.

“Room service!”

Simon opened the door to the steward; he stood there with a chair under his arms. By this time the blinds had been closed and the table had been set up with a white candle alight in the middle of it, visible to the open door.

“Sir, it is hotel policy for no naked flames in the rooms’, I am going to have to ask you to extinguish it.”

"Sure." Simon took the chair and slammed the door in the face of the steward.

The chairs scraped on the wooden floor as each person moved round to make more space for the missing chair.

Simon was unsure on what to do from here, so he carefully followed Pamela's instructions.

"Each of you put your hands on the table; your little fingers should be touching. We need to create a ring of energy; the spirits we call today will draw off that." Pamela muttered as the others waited to be told what else to do.

Simon's heart started to beat more erratic than it had before; he was scared, he could see on the faces of the others, especially Josie, that they all felt the same. He was convinced that this was affecting him and Josie more because they were the ones that had actually encountered the coach; they were scared that calling this Henry Schnieber would cause more trouble than it was worth. Then he thought about that woman in the park and the curse that was upon him, he soon changed his train of thought.

"What else can we do?" Jake asked, seemingly wanting to do more than just sit there and wait.

"You can be quiet until it is time for you to speak." Pamela may be eccentric, but she had a sharp tongue, she wasn't laid back like most other eccentric people.

Pamela muttered a little prayer of protection and called for the spirits of Henry Schnieber and Audrina. She had already been informed of what was needed and how dangerous this little venture was going to be over the phone. Pamela was very good at her job and no matter how she hated it she always delivered it to the highest bidder, no matter the risk.

"Henry, if you are here; make the flame on the candle flicker?"

There was no flicker, but a loud knock, coming from the right hand side of the room near the writing bureau. It made everyone jumped except for Pamela, and Collette screamed.

“Someone has just stood next to me.” Collette claimed, with horror in her face.

“Course someone just stood next to you, it’s a séance; are you going to be screaming like this all the way through cu’s if you are I would rather you leave.” Pamela said rather sternly, she hated it when people do things like that.

Collette’s eye widened, she didn’t like Pamela and this just made her dislike her even more.

Suddenly, out of nowhere another loud bang and the flame on the candle rose up that high and that hot it melted the large church candle in seconds. The two lamps that were on the bedside table flew off and hit the opposite wall with such force that they shattered into small pieces. The telephone for the room rang, no one got up to get it, and everyone was too scared to move, glued to their seats. They knew that it was going to get bad, but Simon didn’t realized quite how bad it would get. Then Simon’s mobile phone rang, as did Jake’s, Collette’s, Josie’s and Pamela’s. Simon reached into his pocket and pulled out his phone. He answered it and slowly put it to his ear, there was no voice, just static. The phones carried on ringing but stopped as Simon disconnected the call, all the phones then went dead. Their batteries immediately drained with no life to them whatsoever.

Then the TV switched itself on, there was no programme, just white noise and snow. Through the TV came a strained quiet voice. . . “Auuudriiiina!”

“Henry, you have proved your point, there is no need for this kind of behaviour to carry on!” Pamela said assertively.

Just then another voice came out the TV, Just as quiet, just as strained. . . “NO!”

Then the TV blew up, sparks and smoke came out the back, the screen went black.

The pictures on the wall shook and fell to the ground, the glass in the frames breaking instantly. The spot lights on the ceiling each turned on and off, then, one by one, they exploded.

Josie's face was of pure fear, tiny shards of glass that had aggressively been thrown from the ceiling lights scattered the table and caused tiny red scratches on the hands and faces of the people sat around the table.

Just like someone was using a very sharp implement the wooden floor around the table and where these people were sitting was being scratched into a circle. Symbols that no one knew about were being etched onto the laminate floor boards too. All, including Pamela was screaming at this point, they knew this was going to be bad, but they didn't know this could happen. Simon and the others tried desperately to get off their chairs, but they couldn't, they were stuck where they sat. The room suddenly went dark; pitch black, not even the light from outside could penetrate the windows.

"What the hell is that?" Said Collette, scared out her wits.

"I don't know," muttered Pamela.

A dark figure in the corner of the room didn't look like any kind of ghost or human any one of them had seen before. This figure was rather twisted, small in height and very bony. The group heard a gargling sound, almost as if it was trying to speak, but couldn't get its words out. It shuffled itself towards Simon and the rest of the group; the screams coming from around the table were ear splitting. Then, three very loud bangs were heard and this scurrying little being, evil or not, ran off back into its corner and once again the sun beamed through the blinds.

Simon thought that would be a relief but as the place lit back up a very large and bulky figure stood in middle of the room. The screaming ceased; they all knew who it was, including Pamela, even though she had not seen his profile, she sensed him immediately. Automatically, everyone removed their hands from one another's and off the table. Pamela thought that in doing so it may drain the energy in the room and eradicate Henry who was looking rather pleased with himself.

The colour drained from the faces of most the people in the room and Simon too was in shock, none of them expected this to happen or turn out quite the way it had.

Simon's attention was turned to Josie who thought at that moment in time it would be a good idea to try and counteract the binding spell that kept them around the table. She muttered some Latin words that made no sense whatsoever to the rest of the team. Unfortunately, Henry knew exactly what she was doing and in the time it took to think about it, Henry was there, right behind her.

"Josephine Hadley? Ever wonder why I spared you." Henry's voice sounded distant, even though he was right there, he knew that his life now belonged to the spirit world, but that didn't make any difference; he'd got the upper hand and he was enjoying himself. He appeared like he had just jumped a century or two, still wearing the same suit that he died in, still with the same old fashioned hair style; his dark eyes seemed to match his personality perfectly.

Josie stopped her little chant the moment her name was mentioned. Tears ran down her cheeks and she looked at the rest of the people at the table, her eyes were begging for help.

"You have a gift, a gift that I gave you on the day you decided to peer into my carriage; pretty stupid thing to do wasn't it?"

With blubbering and frightful tears, Josie agreed, nodding her head slightly.

"There is something that you can do, and judging by the fact that you are still alive, you have yet to discover it."

Disillusioned, Josie was mystified. "W. . .what is it?" She stammered.

"You can use your energy to draw up spirits; I want you to drawer up Audrina."

"It will kill me." It wasn't a question, but Henry seemed to take it as one.

"Yes, but if you don't do this, I will kill all of you. You do want to protect your granddaughter, don't you?"

Josie looked directly at Collette whose eyes were begging her not to do it, Collette would much rather die than watch her gran do this for her, but then she could not condemn the rest of the team to death either.

"Gran?" Collette muttered with tears and a broken voice.

"Will you go away if I do this and lift the curse that is on Simon?" Asked Josie, the desperation in her voice was quite clear.

He bent down so his pale, ghostly lips were almost touching her neck. He gently moved her grey hair to behind her left ear and though he never took his dead eyes off Simon, he whispered, "yes."

Simon could see straight through that evil smirk, he knew Henry was lying.

That is all that Josie needed to hear, she had to save her granddaughter from the onslaught of this evil man. She was not thinking straight, but in spite of that, she agreed.

"What do I have to do?"

"Close your eyes and use your soul to call for her, do so clearly and your death will not be in vain."

Josie looked straight in the eyes of Collette. Briefly, Collette stopped crying.

"Never forget how much I love you; tell your mother and father I said I'm sorry."

As Josie closed her eyes, Collette reached out her hand. "Gran! Gran! No, no, no, no, no." As Josie's body slumped on the table, Collette sobbed for her dead grandmother.

For Josie however, the room had changed. It broke down into a different world, a world that Josie had never known. It was dark and the air around her was thick.

Disturbed people tried to grab hold of her, like zombies from the world above. This was not heaven or hell; if she had to guess she would say that it was purgatory. She looked up, there were no stars, she looked down and the ground was not solid, it was like a dark, silvery liquid that was stable enough to walk on. She came to some large wooden gates, like the gates one would expect to see at medi-evil castles. People seemed desperate to get over these gates, forty-fifty foot high and they were falling, their souls dissipating half way down to the ground and suddenly they were seen again at the top, fighting to come over the gate again.

The gates opened to let her in. All she could hear were the groans of the tortured souls, never able to let go and never able to move on, stuck in their own hell, desperate to try and find a way out.

As she walked through this terrible place, she called out the name, "Auuudriiina!" and realized at that moment, the sound that came out of the TV in the hotel room was not the voice of Henry, as they had all assumed, but her own, calling out for the woman that was keeping Henrys ghost alive.

She called out again and stopped dead when the scene had changed, from the dreadful callings of hell to a dark, dank road, still there were no stars, but the ground was more like a wet tar mac. The occasional wooden shack littered the sides of the road, like small American houses that had been abandoned for decades. The stench of rotting wood and flesh filled the air. High pitched giggles could be heard though there was no way of knowing where they were coming from or what was making them. She could only imagine that they came from the same kind of creature that came into the hotel room when it went deathly dark. Eyes were staring upon her from the twisted bodies that would once have been men; now nothing more than demons, lurking in the dark, waiting to pounce on the nearest unsuspecting victim only for them to also be turned into one of these dark and gruelling creatures of their world.

"Auuuudriiiina!" Josie called again; scared out of her wits; her nerves were gone; she shook from head to toe in fear.

She called out again, desperate to find her. Josie had no idea what would happen to her once she had found her, but it had to be better than this; she was a Christian through life so she knew she didn't belong in this kind of place. There was a place in heaven for her, she believed that and didn't give up, her faith was stronger than ever.

Josie built up the courage to take a look in one of these old shacks; she took a step up to the old creaky wooden porch and called out Audrina's name as she popped her head around the door, too scared to venture any further. To Josie the shack was empty, but to the soul that lived there it was not and neither were all the other shacks that seemed to go on forever down this dark, long straight road.

Josie kept trying these shacks, each with their own soul and each soul with their own stories. Eventually, Josie came to a shack stood on its own. There was something different about the place, a different type of air seemed to surround it. She knew that if this was not the one she was looking for then, this could turn out to be very bad indeed. However, she knew she had to take the chance.

Josie walked up to the house from the creaky wooden steps that led up to it and opened the door. Inside, she called out Audrina's name again, and this time instead of it being empty she saw a glimpse of a soul as it practically flew past the door leading to the other room. Reluctantly, she entered the house, knowing that there was someone here that might be able to help.

"Audrina?" Josie called softly.

Josie built up the nerve to walk into the next room, the old wooden door, was closed and heavy to pull open. She walked into a room that would once have been a kitchen, an old aga oven and other household items were in a state to total disrepair. The floor was covered in mud and old dead leaves decaying, the stench was unrecognisable and terrible; there was no good in this house, only death and misery.

In the far end of the room was an old table, benches surrounded it rather than chairs, and there sitting up the table was a figure; her hair was long and dark, knotted in all directions and she looked as filthy as the rest of the house. She had her head in her hands facing the surface of the table; her hair hung down like vines in a tropical rain forest.

"Audrina?"

No answer.

"Audrina, my name is. . ."

"I know who you are, you don't belong here, get out." She said in a rather soft but raspy voice.

Josie was taken aback; her words did not suit the tone of her voice.

"Audrina, I have been sent here from Henry."

By this, she stirred; twisting herself into shape. Her head lifted, still covered over by her long, filthy hair. She smiled and all Josie could see was a set of black, broken teeth.

"Henry wants me?" Her voice was excitable almost like she had an agenda of her own.

"Yes, his soul can not rest until you go to him; he's killing people."

"Where is he?"

"He responded to a séance, he is going to kill my friends and family if I don't bring you back."

Audrina's smile broadened, and the house where they stood broke down bit by bit and changed into a brighter room, a room that looked almost brand new. One would not think it is the same place, yet it was, just clean and bright and the atmosphere was happier, Josie realised in this place, the environments are attached the mood and thoughts of the souls living in them.

"Then we must oblige him." A new prim and proper Audrina said her teeth had turned from the black that they were to a lovely white set. Her hair was clean and brushed, hanging loose to the middle of her back. Her dress was long but bright. Her complexion was no longer dirty; she looked as fresh as a new born butterfly.

She headed towards the front door, but Josie wasn't too eager to go back out to the dark road with all those demons there, waiting, lurking around corners, ready to create more mayhem. As Audrina moved towards the door and opened it, instead of the dark street that Josie was expecting, a bright light shone through, almost blinding Josie. Audrina ushered her though and followed her before shutting the door behind them.

~#~

Everything had happened so fast and Jake didn't quite understand what was going on around him. He understood as much as the others did, but still, one minute they were performing a séance, and the next all hell broke loose. What on earth was he supposed to think? He had sat there quiet ever since Pamela told him to shut up. He just didn't know what to do or what to say; stunned is probably the better word for how he felt, stunned and scared.

Josie was slumped dead on the table, Collette was crying over her, not letting go of her still warm hand. Simon's eyes were full of fear and so wide open Jake thought that they could pop out of their sockets at any minute. Pamela was praying, muttering words as she was asking for help and protection with tears running down her cheeks. Her mascara had smudged terribly, causing black streaks to run down her face. The ghost of Henry Schnieber had gone from the full apparition that they all witnessed earlier and now he was circling above the table like a heavy storm cloud ready to explode at any given moment.

For Jake it almost seemed biblical when the ghosts of Audrina and Josie stepped into the room. A bright light surrounded them as they walked in from a different spiritual plain.

As soon as Henry sensed Audrina's presence, he appeared back to his human form.

"I've missed you, my darling; I could not rest without you." Henry said with more compassion in his eyes than Jake could ever think possible, especially from a soul like his.

"Henry, I've been waiting, waiting to tell you this." There was a pause as Henry could not move his eyes away from the depths of Audrina big brown eyes.

They moved in closer and before Audrina could finish her sentence, their lips gently touched and they kissed. At this point Jake was beginning to think that they might all come out of this alive after all, apart from Josie.

~#~

Josie

Josie knew that what she needed to do was done and she belonged on earth no more. The door to the spiritual plain opened again; she knew that she was going to a better place to claim her space in heaven, only this time she was not afraid. She had a very peaceful and uplifting feeling; she could be no more scared of that door than she could be of her own home, but Josie could not leave without saying goodbye. She turned to face Collette, her granddaughter and mouthed ‘I love you,’ smiled and made her way through to a world that she felt she already knew.

~#~

Collette

Collette cried until she had no more tears, she was happy because she believed her grandmother was going to a better place than this, where she could be safe and happy. Nevertheless, it’s still hard to say goodbye to someone you love.

~#~

Pamela

Pamela had a feeling that something like this was going to happen. She didn’t know for sure as divination is not a part of her gift. She didn’t know or like Josie so secretly Pamela couldn’t really care less, she was just glad that it didn’t happen to her. But then, Henry wouldn’t kill her would he? After all, she was the only medium there. Now she was the only one that could put their souls at rest in the place where they were meant to be.

She had no idea what was going to happen next.

~#~

Henry

Henry felt alive for the first time in over one hundred and fifty years. He had standing in front of him the love of his life, the woman he could've spent the rest of his life with. His heart filled up with the love he thought he had lost, his energy began to shine. But his soul was still dark, that was something that would never change. He and Audrina looked into each others eyes and Henry held her cheek in the palm of his hand, all that was in his eyes for this woman was love. A love that Henry did not know was not reciprocated. Their lips met, they kissed, but Audrina's kiss had been poisoned with the misery of time. She had been miserable for over a century, not because she couldn't be with Henry, but because she hated him that much she could not get him out her mind and it turned her bitter, very bitter. Her kiss, his kiss was poison and she knew it. Unfortunately Henry did not, so when they kissed his jaw dropped, he felt how she felt, how she had never loved him. How it was him that was always heckling her to be with him, how it was her father that was quick to palm her off to him because Henry had power and money. He was forced to look back at the times where she tried to get away from him, he always just thought she was playing hard to get. His ego was too big to think she never really wanted him; she hated him, he scared her, it was circumstances that brought them together and it was his ego and murderous arrogance that brought them together again. He would not give up, not on her, he couldn't, he loved her too much but his soul was cursed with the fire that murdered him, hence the reason why people burned at the sight of him. Audrina knew she had to put a stop to it, because there was no way that Henry would.

Henry looked upon Audrina with shock in his eyes; she looked back with a knowing and mocking smile. She knew how this would destroy him, and destroy him it did. He fell apart under his own burning curse, a whirlwind of dust encircled the room, fire bubbling the ceiling and the heat was tremendous. It seemed to last forever, but in reality it lasted just minutes, Henry's cursed soul rained down and landed like little grains of sand hitting the sketched wooden floor.

~#~

Collette

Collette beamed, though the spell was still in force, they were still not able to move from off that table. Collette, Pamela, Jake and Simon all sat in awe of what they had just witnessed. Collette felt that her life was no longer in any danger; she didn't feel threatened by Audrina.

~#~

Audrina

Audrina was brought back to destroy Henry, she had lived in limbo for over a century simply for this reason and now she had destroyed him she was almost happy. Looking up at her were four people, four living, breathing people, and Audrina wanted to stay, she wanted her life back. There was no way that she was going back there, to a world that didn't really exist but in the mind of the beholder. She noticed that the hard work had already been done for her, they were already stuck to their seats so keeping them still was not going to be hard.

In Audrina's life, she studied witchcraft and was almost caught, but luckily for her, she was not. It was at that point though that made her think about how dangerous it was and that she had to give it up. She did, but she never forgot what she learned. Although, if she was going to do this, then there could not be any witnesses. She had spent all that time in the most miserable place. . .her own mind. She could not spend the rest of eternity with that kind of misery on her shoulders, she had to eradicate it. She knew exactly what to do. Her eyes narrowed and Simon, along with Collette, Pamela and Jake knew there was something wrong, they thought that they were safe now that Henry was gone; they could not be more wrong. In the world where Audrina had come, death was contagious, a disease that she brought with her. With determination in her unbeaten heart and death in her eyes she simply touched the head of Simon, Jake and Pamela. Each of them instantly turned blue, their breathing stopped quite rapidly and their eyes sank into the back of their heads, their mouths opened wide like they had all been killed by pure sadness and fear all rolled into one. Jake slumped onto the back of his chair, Simon fell forward onto the table and Pamela fell off the chair, hitting the floor with a thump.

Collette saw this and though it may have been a little bit of a late reaction due to shock, she screamed; her mind went blank, she could not think of a thing to say, she just screamed and screamed until her throat became hoarse. Tears streamed down her cheeks, she wanted to ask why? But before she could she felt the effects of the soft words Audrina had began to mutter, a spell to swap their souls. Just like Collette was breathing out the smoke off a cigarette, her soul left her body. Collette's eyes went blank as her ghost stood by and watched how Audrina sat in her seat and took over the shell that used to be Collette's body.

Collette was no longer Collette but Audrina.

Audrina sat just for a minute in her new body, getting used to the feel of it. She liked it, in fact she loved it. Her skin was smooth, her features, pretty. Her eyes were alive. She run her fingers through her hair and wiggled her toes in her designer low heeled shoes. She pursed her lips and ran her tongue across her teeth. She admired her newly manicured fingernails, took in one deep breath and with one swift action, waved her hand over the circle to cause a break in the floor that was holding her to her chair. Audrina sat back and lifted her new body off the chair and made her way to the door. She held on to the handle, just for a second while she felt the grip of her new hand. She walked out of the door and rather than take the lift she took the stairs, practically skipping, she almost jumped the last step. She walked through the foyer, passing the reception desk.

"Excuse me, have you finished with the room?" The receptionist asked.

"Yes, they'll be out soon." Trying to cover herself, she heard her voice for the first time. It felt like it rang.

She walked out the revolving door and into the night time, she walked down the street in awe of the way the world had changed in the past one hundred years.

~#~

Epilogue

Collette

Collette knew that the way the world had changed in the last century would mean that Audrina wouldn't last five minutes or at least that is what she hoped. She waited in the sidelines, hoping one day Audrina would slip up and Collette would get her body back. At least that is what she prayed for.

The End.

Printed in Great Britain
by Amazon.co.uk, Ltd.,
Marston Gate.